OUR BEACH

REBECCA SMITH

Illustrated by ZOE WARING

HarperCollins *Children's Books*

Over the sand dunes
and through the long grass.

Sun on the **sea**,
      shining brightly like glass.

Two pairs of feet
side by side on the sand,

Granddad and I
at our beach, hand in hand.

Finding fish,
crabs and shrimp
in the pools
by the rocks.

"Oh, Granddad," I say.
"You've got soggy socks."

Off come the socks left to dry in the sun,

Paddling barefoot
is so much more fun.

Combing the seashore
for **seashells**
and **stones,**

Treasures that one time
were sea-creatures' homes.

KNOCK-KNOCK!

It's the door.
But who could it be?

"Come back here, Granddad,
come back
to the sea!"

Granny is cooking.
I can hear her voice sing.

And Granddad returns with a big ball of string...

…The kite string unspools.

It soars up to the skies,

The ribbons flip-flap

as the kite ducks and dives.

Mischievous seagulls
squawk loudly in flight,

Time for the next thing!
Let's reel in the kite.

"Granddad, remember
the castle we made?

Let's build a bigger one –
I've got the spade."

Stack it up **high**!

"Build it up tall, Granddad.

Then let's add a flag
so it touches the sky!"

The afternoon comes and it's time for some cricket.
Away from the castle
to find us a wicket.

"Here, Granddad, just here!
This bit is flat.

You *always* bowl
and I *always* bat."

SMASH!

And then – plop!

Straight into the sea.

"Let's go and retrieve it,"
says Granddad with glee.

Together, and laughing, we quickly splash in,
The waves lap our bodies
as we start to swim.

Slippery seaweed
    between all my toes,

        The smell of the saltwater
        filling my nose.

Or is that **something else** in the air I can smell?
        Granddad's aware of it,
            sniffing as well.

Granny calls happily,
"Time for our tea!"

We swim to the shore
and then race
from the sea.

Dry ourselves off,
    lift the towels from the floor,

        Hang up the **kite**
            on the back of the door.

Rub off the **sand**
from our toes
and my face,

Tidy the **sitting room**,
leave not a trace.

No sign of our beach when I woke up today.

Granddad called home
from a place
far away.

RING-RING!
RING-RING!

"How is our beach?"

"Oh, Granddad,
when you're not here
it's just a room
with two sofas.

Come back soon!"